characters created by lauren child

KU-060-701

MY Best, BEST Friend

PUFFIN

Charlie and Lola™

Text based on the script written by Carol Noble

Illustrations from the TV animation produced by Tiger Aspect

PUFFIN BOOKS
Published by the Penguin Group: London, New York, Australia,
Canada, India, Ireland, New Zealand and South Africa
Penguin Books Ltd, Registered Offices: 80 Strand, London WC2R 0RL, England

puffinbooks.com

First published 2010
1 3 5 7 9 10 8 6 4 2

I have this little sister Lola.
She is small and very funny.
"Shh, Charlie. You must keep still!
Otherwise our spell will not work!"

Lola has this **friend** Lotta...

"I can smell a Charlie,"
says Lola.

Lotta says,
"You are going
to be turned into a
stinky toad!"

Lola and Lotta are best, best, BEST friends.

They share everything.

Lotta says, "I don't like my orange today.
    It's too... Orange!"

Lola says,
"I don't think I like my banana today.
    It's too banana!
        Let's swap!"

And when Mrs Hanson says,
"Get into pairs"...

...they
ALWAYS
go
TOGETHER.

Lola and Lotta both love looking at the school fishpond.

"What are all those black **wiggly** things?" says Lotta.

"They are **tadpoles**,"
says Lola.
"They turn into **frogs**!"

Lotta says,
"Look at the **tadpoles**!
They are playing
hide-and-seek."

"Look! The big orangey fish is still in bed. He looks sleepy."

Then Lola hears a ringing noise.

BRRING!

BRRING!

"Quick, Lotta, it's the **school bell**."

"Hurry up, Lola."

"Just got to get
my things, Lotta."

When Lola gets to the classroom,
Lotta says,
"This is Evie. She's new!"

"Hello, Evie," says Lola.
"I am Lola."

"We must show Evie where everything is,"
says Lola.
"This is the corridor. And you have to do
walking, not **running**."

"Otherwise you will be told, 'No **running**!'"
says Lotta.

"And these are the **coatpegs** for
hanging up your coat."

"Yes, and you
will probably get one
next to mine,"
says Lotta.

"And this is...
the **wall**,"
says Lola.

"Yes, a **wall**,"
says Lotta.

"Oh," says Evie.

"And this is where we eat our lunch!" says Lola.
"I wish I had something orange."

"I wish I had something yellow,"
says Lotta.

"Let's swap!"
says Evie.

So Lotta and Evie swap.

In the sand pit,
Lotta says,
"I know! Let's **join** them up."

"Shall I **join** up too?"
says Lola.

"No," says Lotta.
"Because then you can come and visit."

"Oh," says Lola.

When we get home from school,
    I say,
      "What's wrong, Lola?"

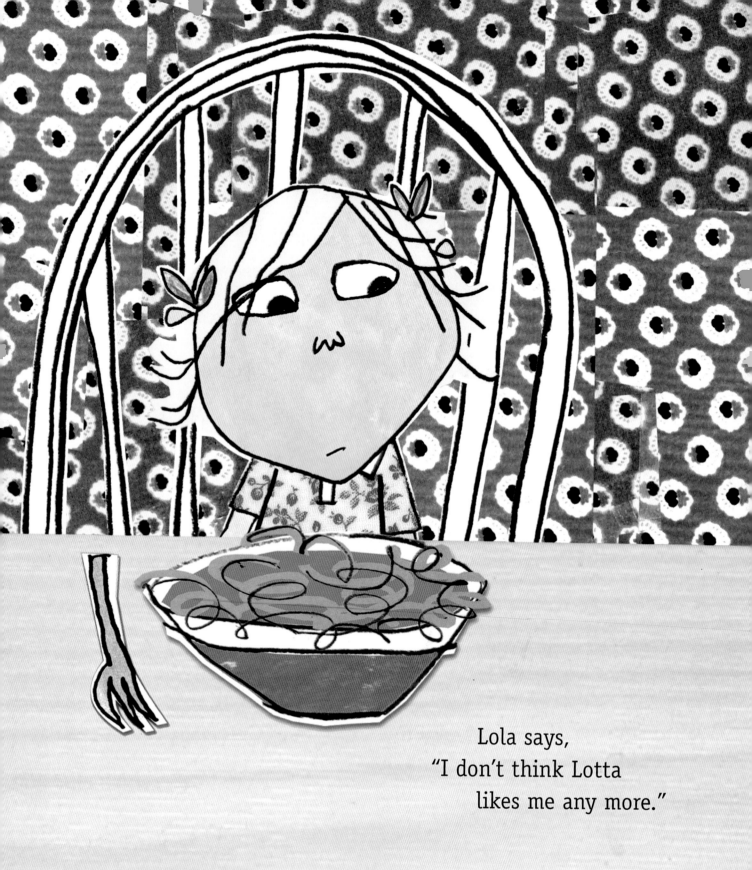

Lola says,
"I don't think Lotta
likes me any more."

And I say,

"But she's
your best friend...

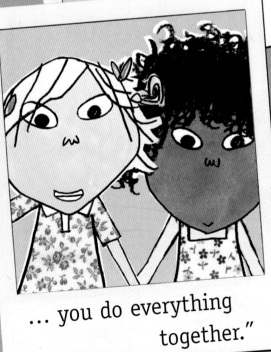

... you do everything together."

"That was ages ago,"
says Lola.

And I say,
"It was only last week.
Perhaps you will be best
friends again tomorrow."

"Do you think so, Charlie?"

The next day, Lola sees
Lotta playing with Evie.

Lotta says,
"Evie, in the world of the pond
live all these **millions** of tiny **tadpoles**
and they are always playing
hide-and-seek."

"I don't think **tadpoles** play **hide-and-seek**," says Evie.

"Hmm," says Lotta. Then she says, "Evie, Mum said you can come to tea."

At bedtime, I say,
    "So how was Lotta today?
Are you best friends again?"

"No," says Lola.
    "Lotta is not my
best, be&t BESTEST
    friend any more."

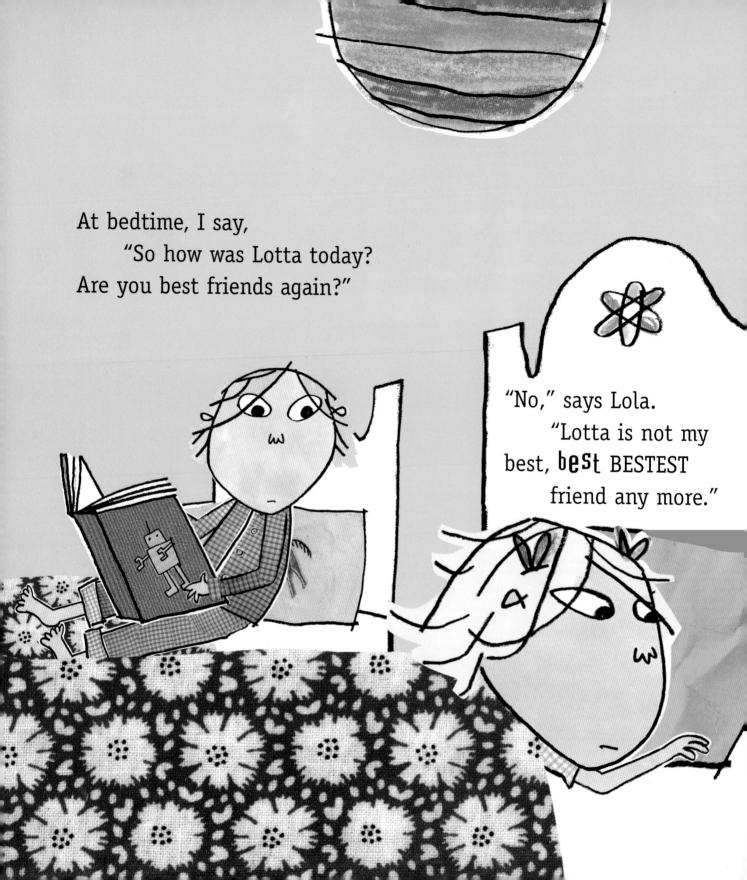

The next day, Marv says,
"Lola seems a bit down
in the dumps."

And I say,
"Yes, she says Lotta has
a new best friend."

And then we have an idea...

... we swing Lola high in the air...

Meanwhile Lotta says, "Maybe the **tadpoles** will wake the big fish up with all their playing and shouting?"

"**Tadpoles** don't shout," says Evie.

"Oh," says Lotta. "Look, there's Lola!"

"Do it again!"
says Lola.

"Lola!" shouts Lotta.
"Do you want to come
and see what's in
the pond?"

Lola says,
    "Ooh, those tadpoles are going
to wake up the big fish with all their shouting!"

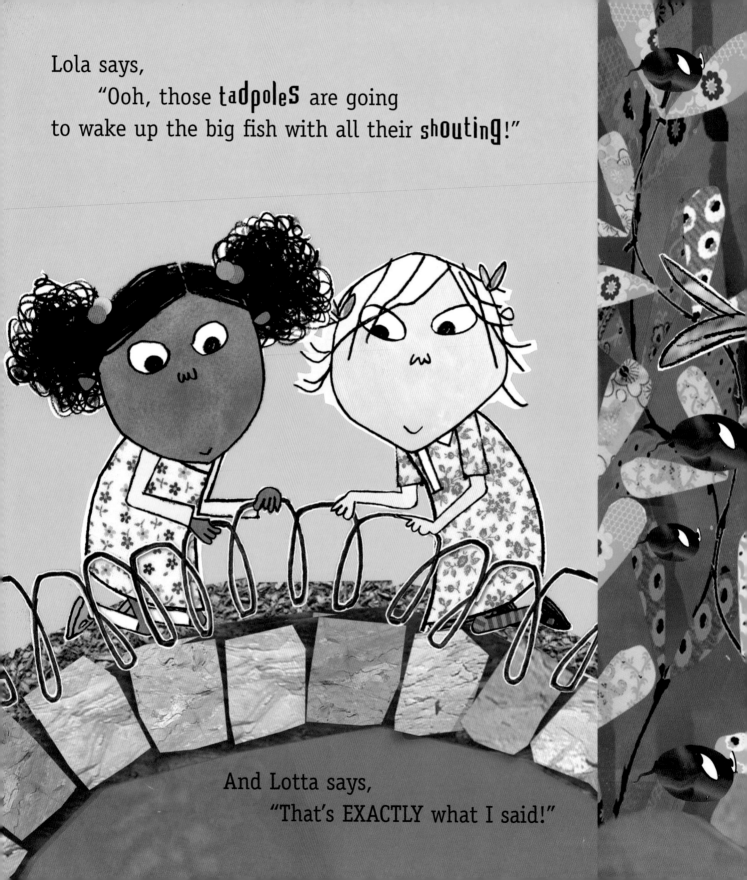

And Lotta says,
    "That's EXACTLY what I said!"

Lotta says,
    "Where's Evie gone?"

"She's over there **playing**,"
    says Lola.

Then Lotta says,
"Lola, I saw Charlie and Marv
swinging you
and it looked really fun."

And Lola says,
"Charlie and Marv, will you give
        my best, best BESTEST friend Lotta a swing?"

"WHHEEE!"